MEL BAY PRESENTS

Christmas Music
for Acoustic Guitar

BY STEPHEN SIKTBERG

A cassette tape of the music in this book is now available. The publisher strongly recommends the use of this cassette tape along with the text to insure accuracy of interpretation and ease in learning.

Foreword

The arrangements in this book are for the guitarist with intermediate to advanced finger-style technique, and can be played on both nylon and steel string instruments. Standard classical guitar notation and symbols are used throughout, with Roman numerals indicating the fret numbers to be barred with the first finger (a fraction before the Roman numeral tells you how many strings to cover in a partial barre).

Several of the pieces require the use of alternate tunings. These include Renaissance lute tuning (tune the third string down to F♯) and drop D tuning (tune the sixth string down to D). In the case of "Silent Night," the sixth string is tuned down to D and the fifth string is tuned down to G.

Special attention should be paid to the recommendations for use of a capo in several of the pieces. Although one can achieve satisfying results without it, the lute-like sound which results from playing in the upper register helps to enhance the Renaissance and baroque flavor of the music.

Contents

Deck The Halls

Deck The Halls

Traditional
Arranged for guitar
by Stephen C. Siktberg

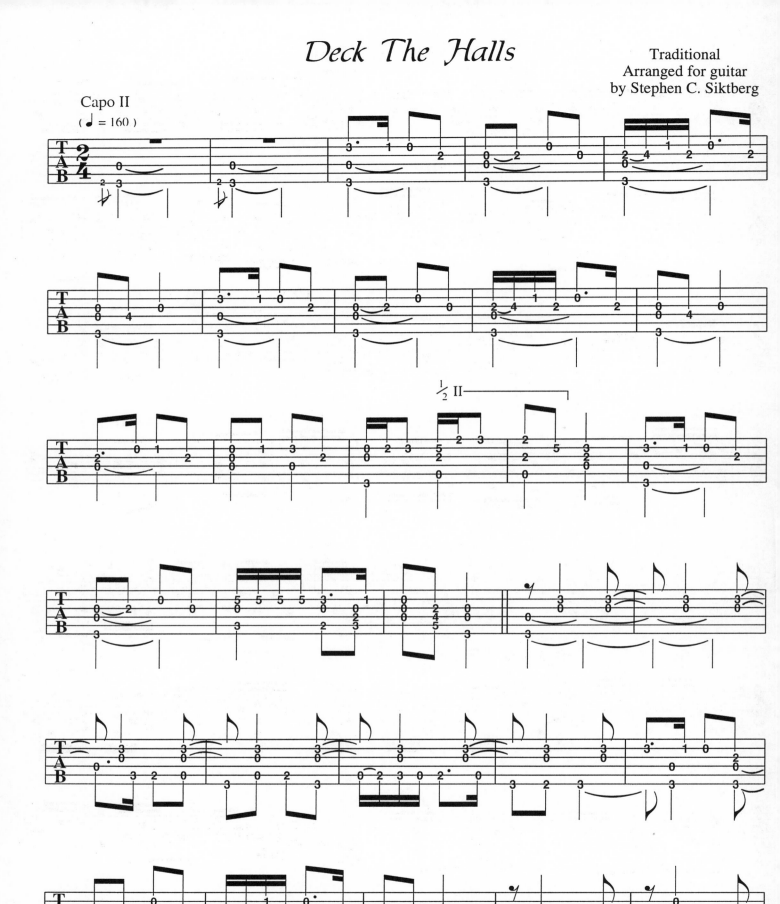

God Rest Ye Merry Gentlemen

Capo III

Moderato Rubato (♩ = 96)

Traditional
Arranged for guitar
by Stephen C. Siktberg

9

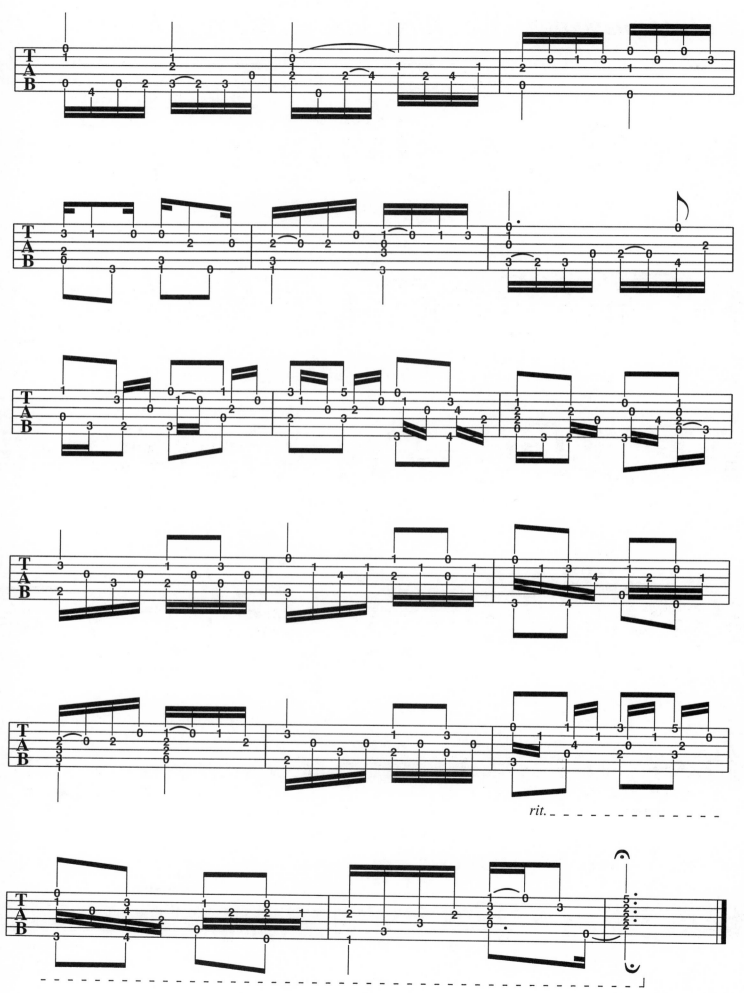

rit. _ _ _ _ _ _ _ _ _ _ _ _ _ _

17

O Tannenbaum/We Wish You a Merry Christmas

Traditional
Arranged for guitar
by Stephen C. Siktberg

18

19

O Tannenbaum/We Wish You a Merry Christmas

Traditional
Arranged for guitar
by Stephen C. Siktberg

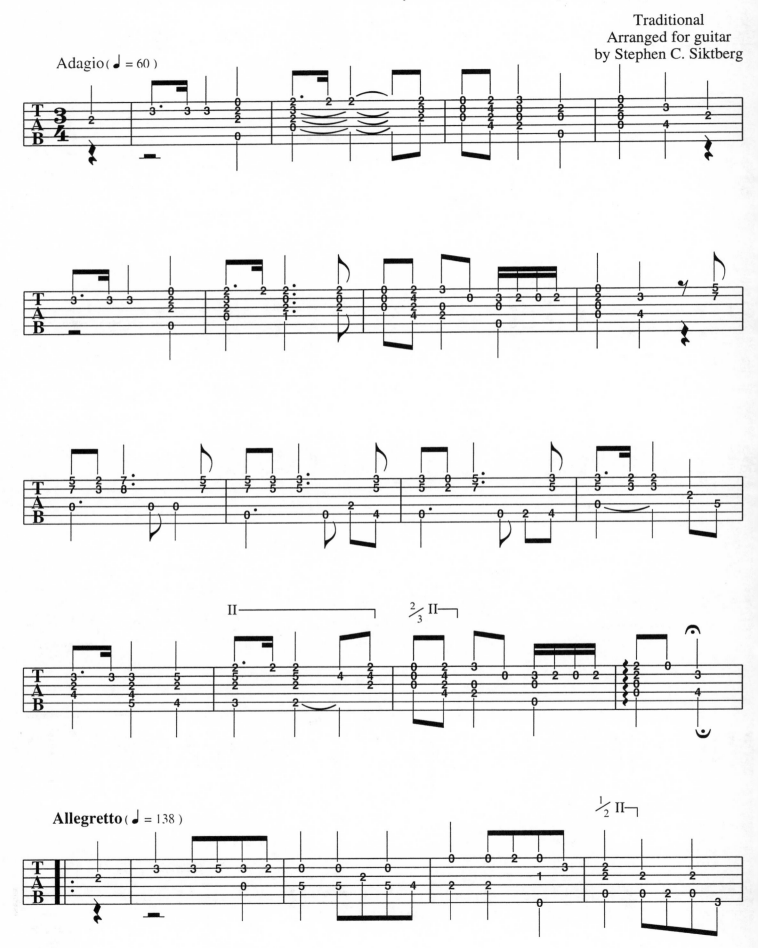

O, Holy Night

Adolphe Adam
Arranged for guitar
by Stephen C. Siktberg

23

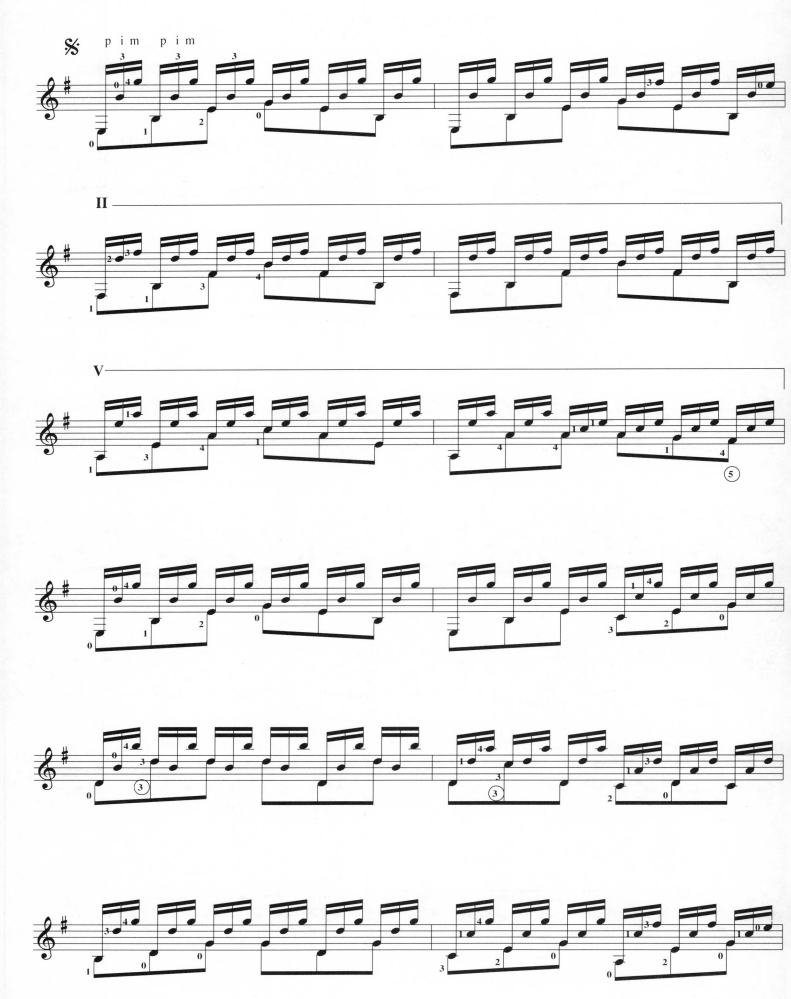

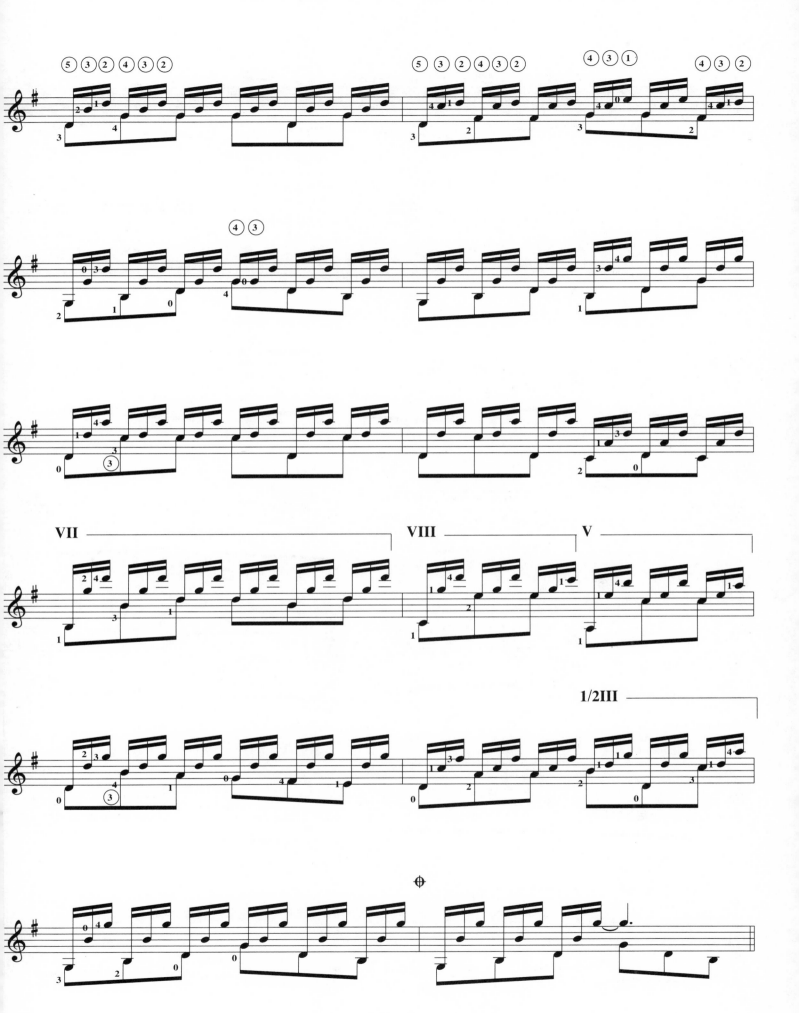

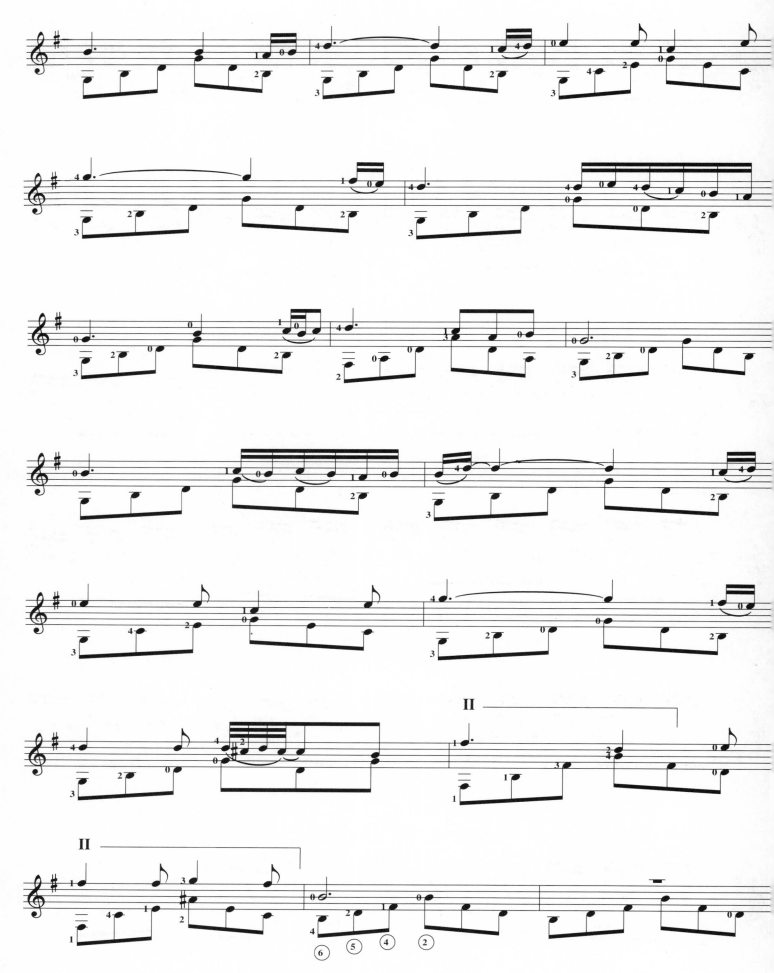

26

D.S. 𝄋 al Coda ⊕

Coda ⊕

2/3 I

p p p i m a

rit − − − − − − − − − − − − −

27

O, Holy Night

Adolphe Adam
Arranged for guitar
by Stephen C. Siktberg

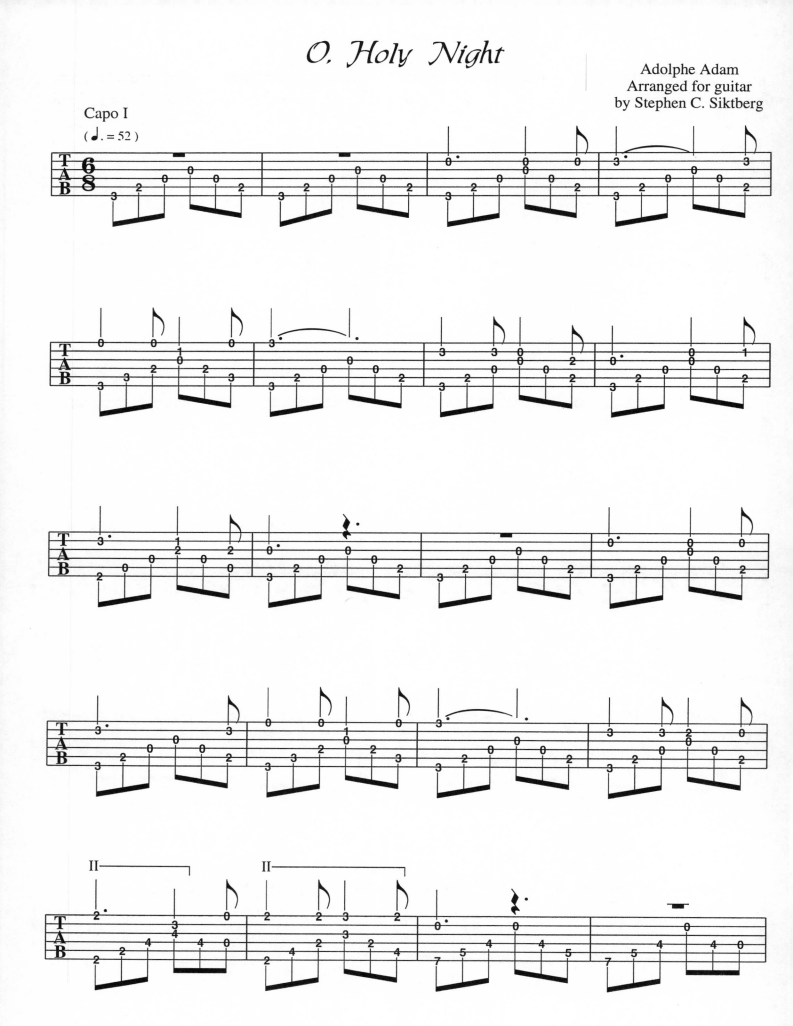

28

O, Little Town of Bethlehem

Lewis H. Redner
Arranged for guitar
by Stephen C. Siktberg

33

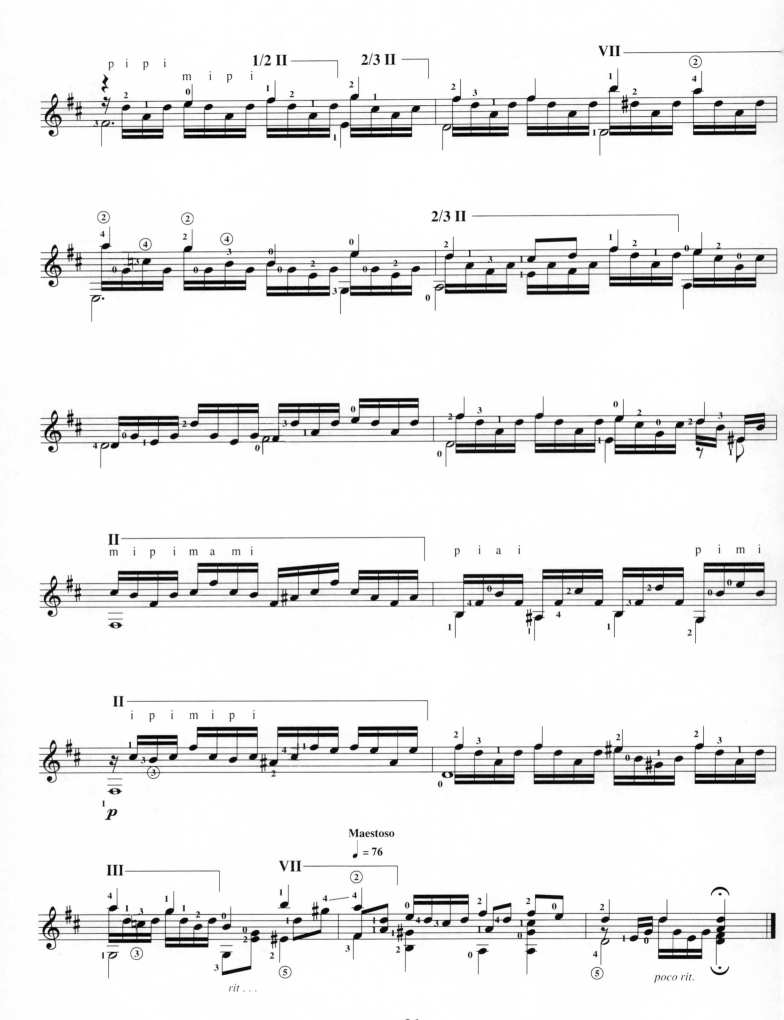

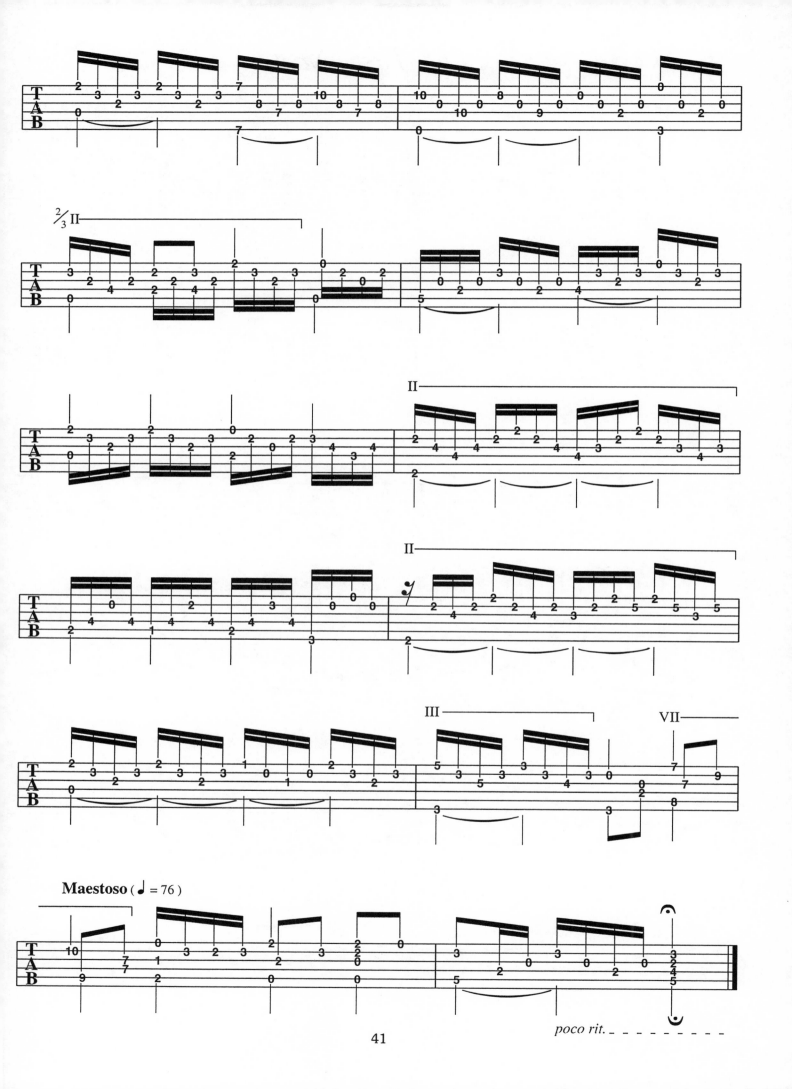

The First Noel

Capo III

Traditional
Arranged for guitar
by Stephen C. Siktberg

44

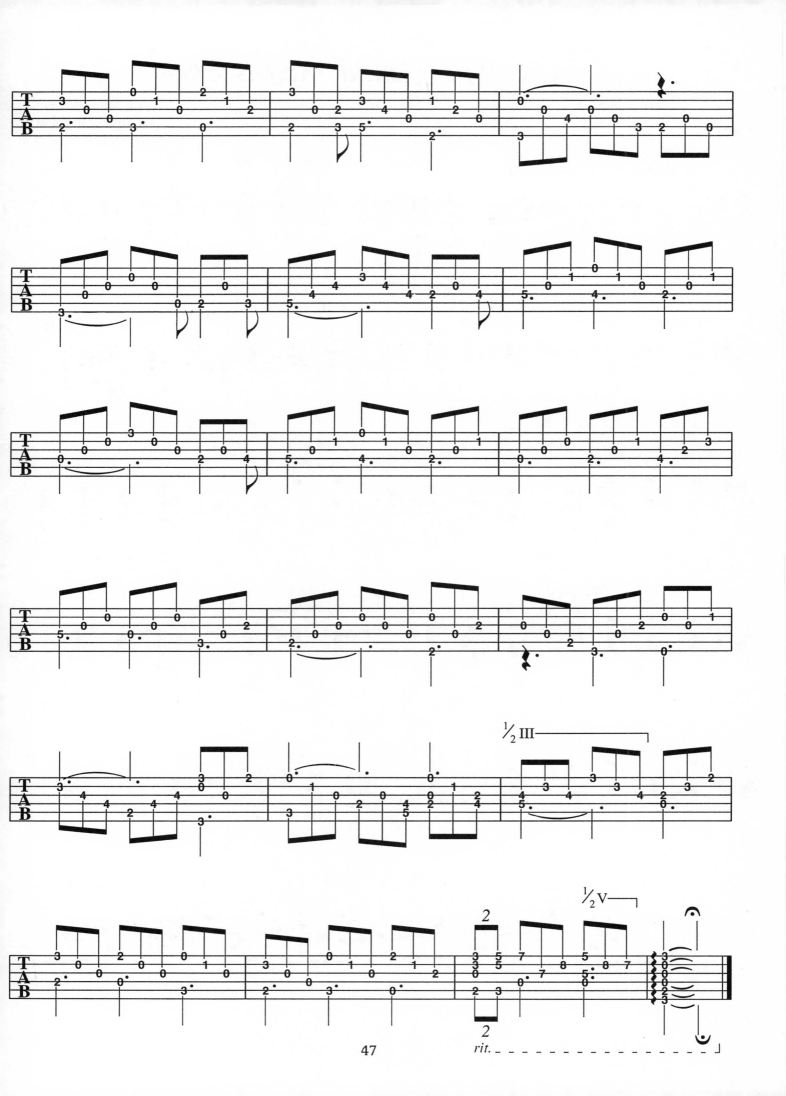

Hark! The Herald Angels Sing

Felix Mendelssohn
Arranged for guitar
by Stephen C. Siktberg

49

Hark! The Herald Angels Sing

Felix Mendelssohn
Arranged for guitar
by Stephen C. Siktberg

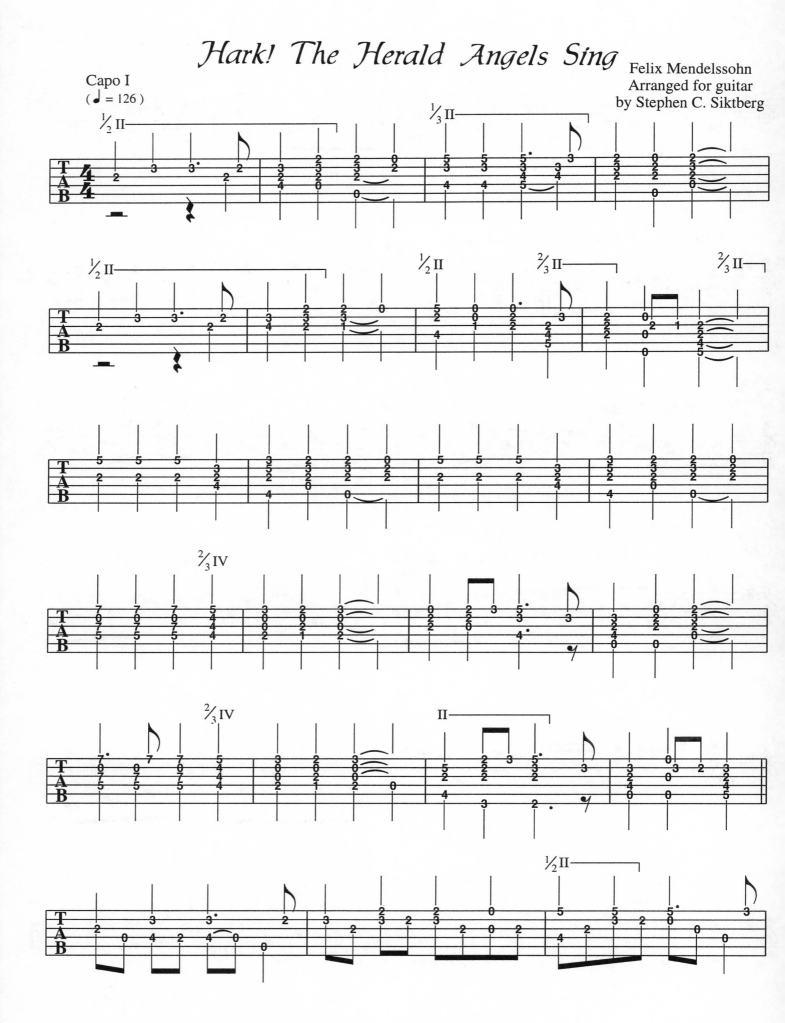

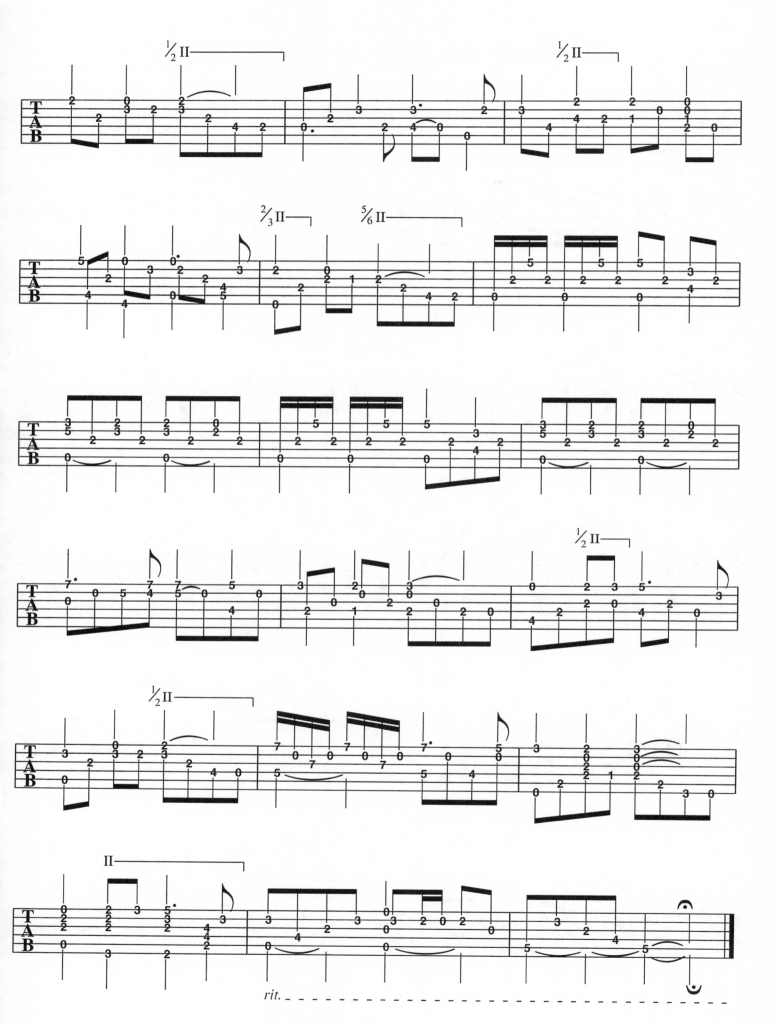

It Came Upon A Midnight Clear

Richard S. Willis
Arranged for guitar
by Stephen C. Siktberg

Capo I

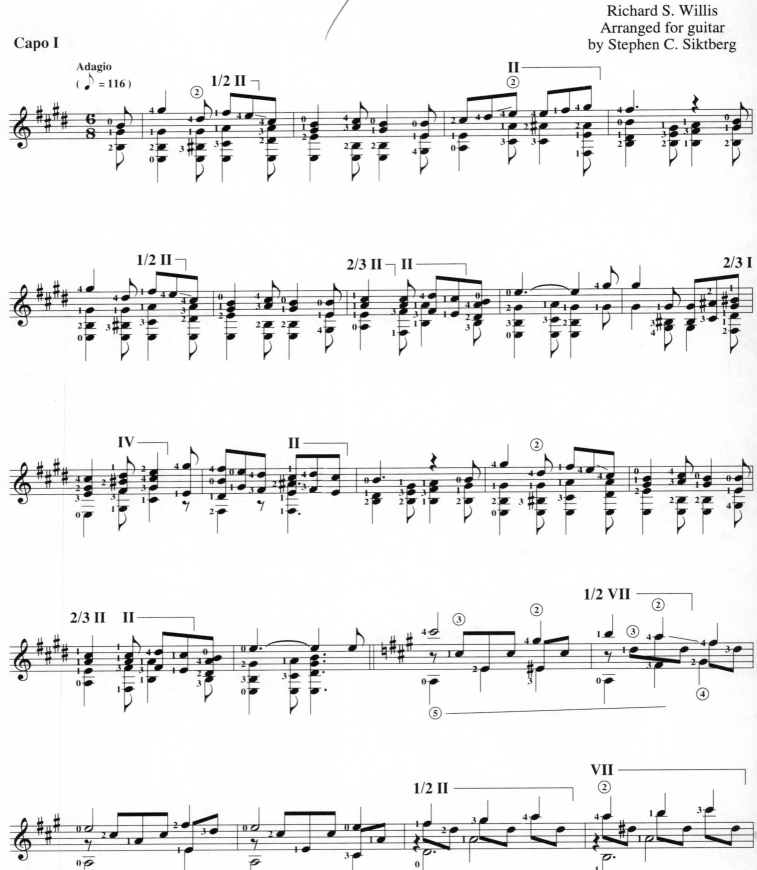

It Came Upon A Midnight Clear

Richard S. Willis
Arranged for guitar
by Stephen C. Siktberg

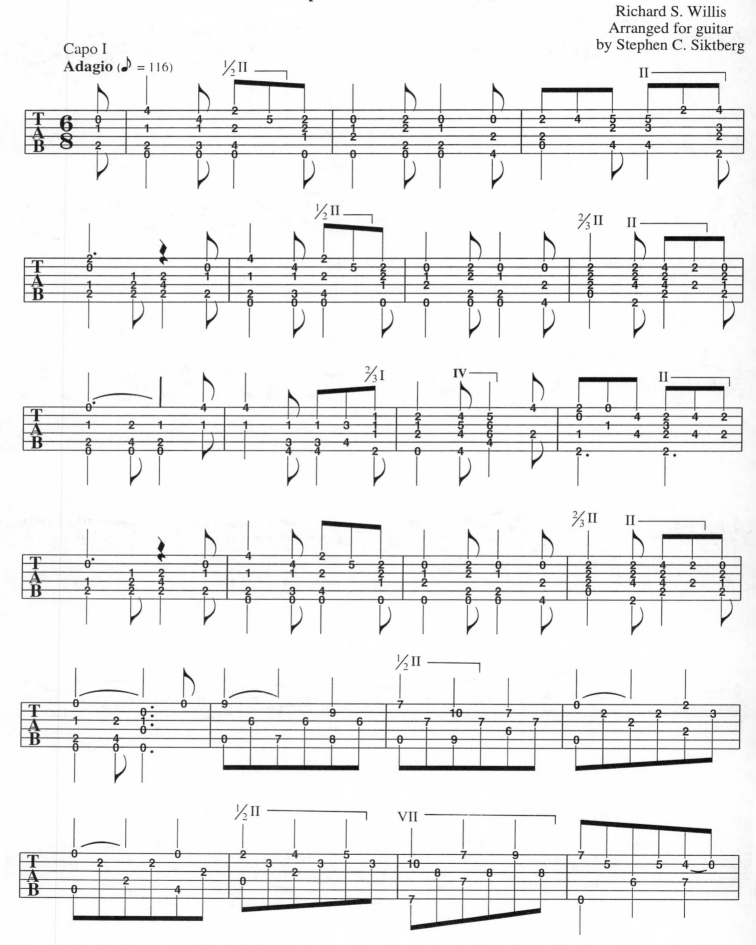

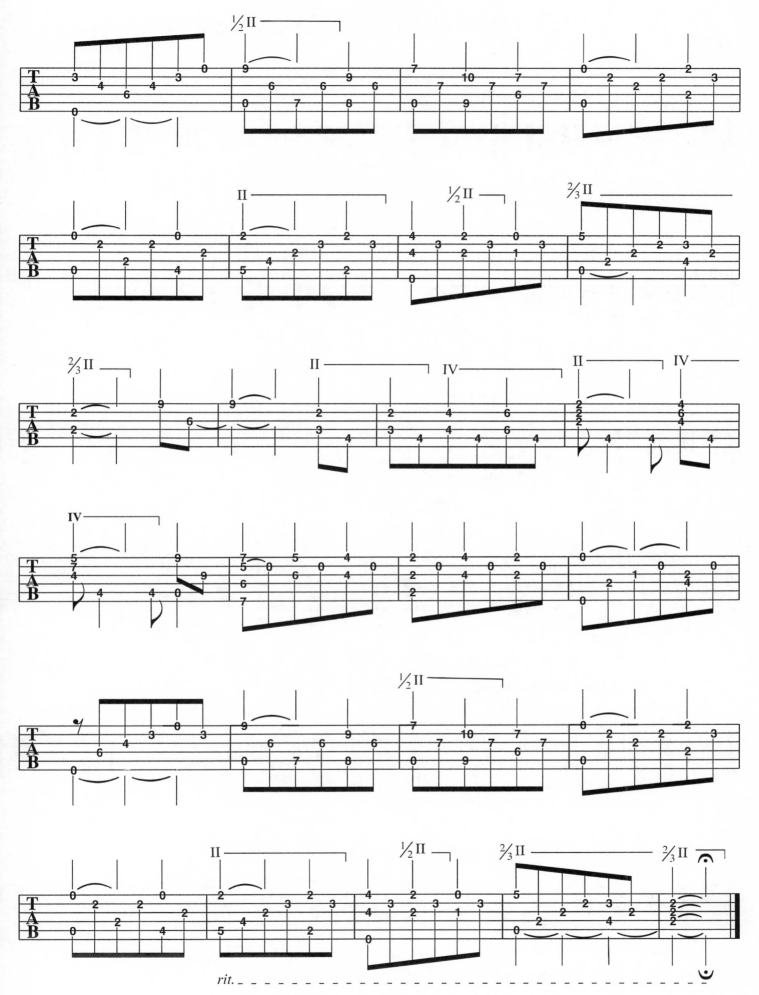

O Come O Come Emmanuel

Traditional
Arranged for guitar
by Stephen C. Siktberg

Capo III

Lo! How A Rose E're Blooming   *Traditional

(*This arrangement is based on Michael Praetorius' harmonization.)

O Come O Come . . .

rit. -

O Come O Come Emmanuel

Traditional
Arranged for guitar
by Stephen C. Siktberg

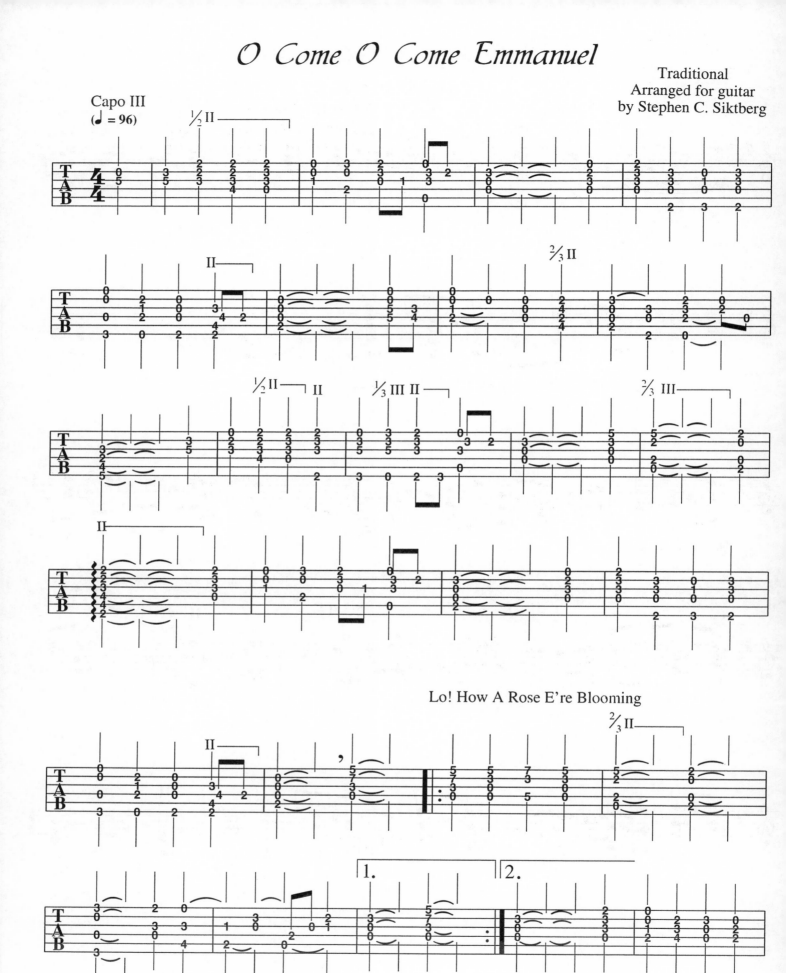

Lo! How A Rose E're Blooming

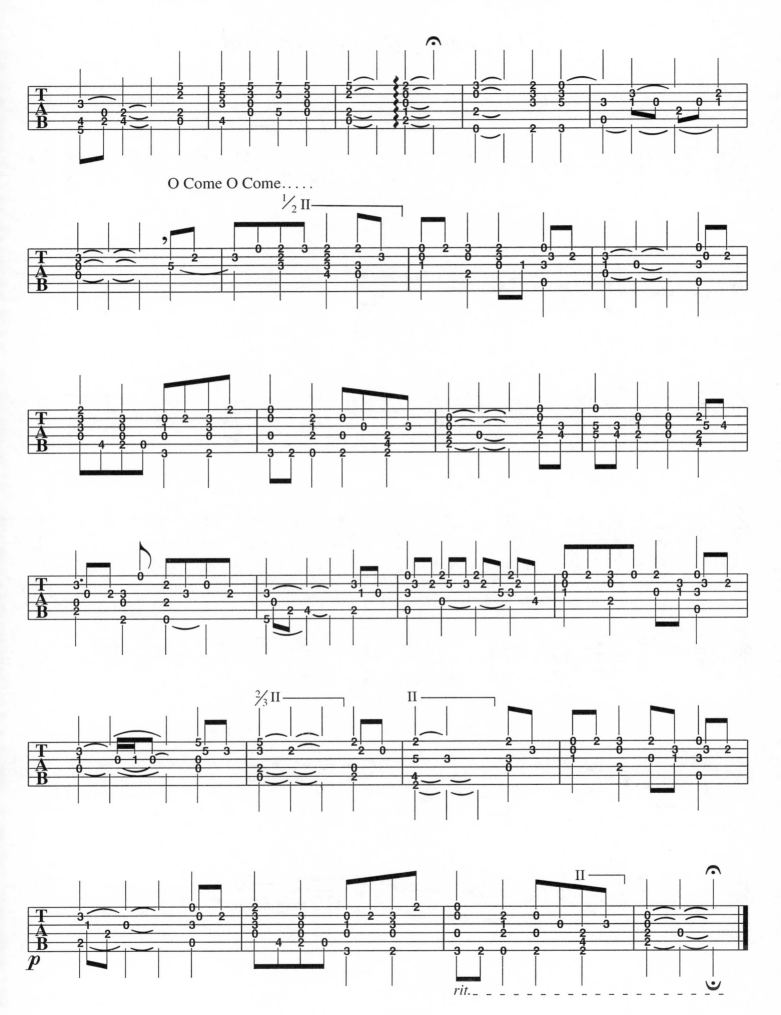

O Come O Come. . . . .

59

O Come, All Ye Faithful

J. F. Wade
Arranged for guitar
by Stephen C. Siktberg

Capo II

(♩ = 132)

O Come, All Ye Faithful

J. F. Wade
Arranged for guitar
by Stephen C. Siktberg

Capo II (♩ = 132)

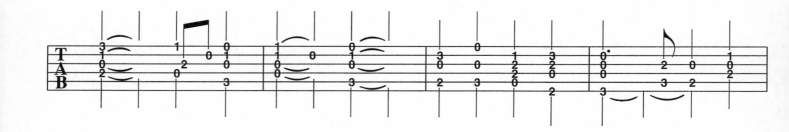

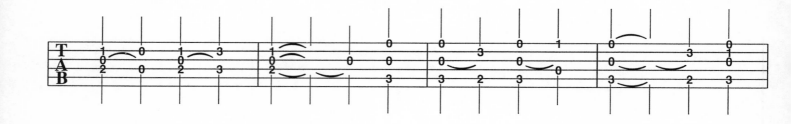

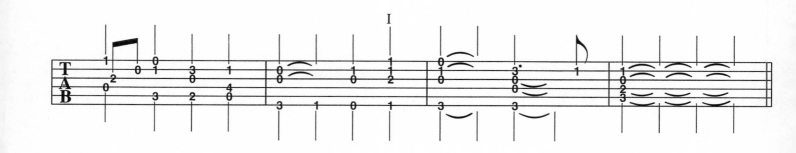

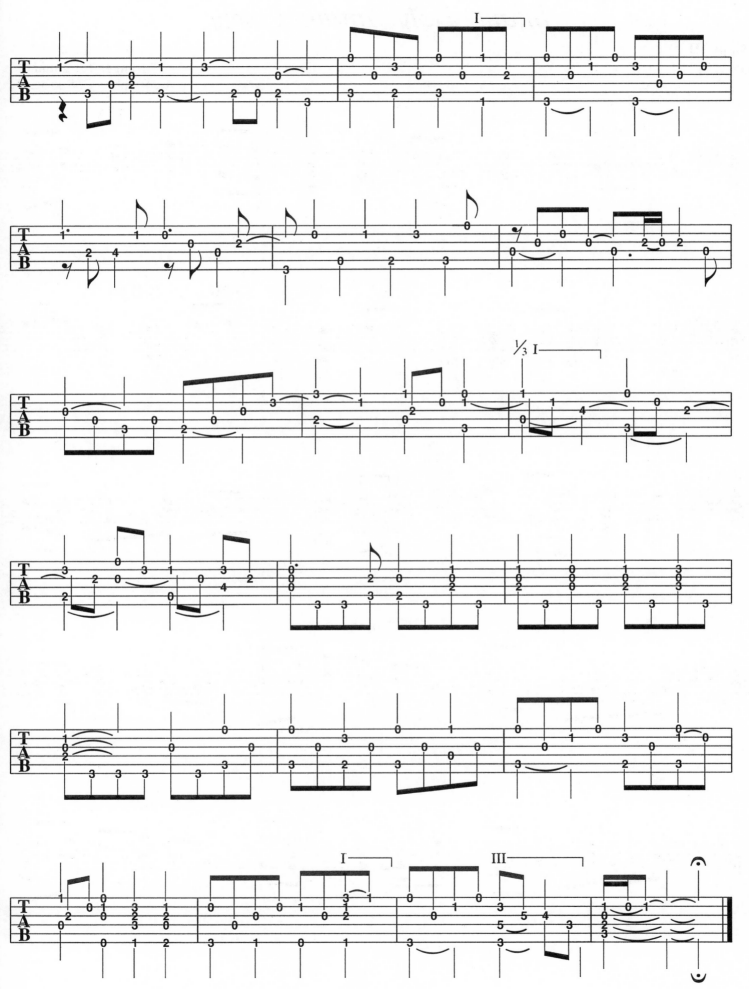

63

Infant Holy, Infant Lowly

Traditional
Arranged for guitar
by Stephen C. Siktberg

64

Infant Holy, Infant Lowly

Traditional
Arranged for guitar
by Stephen C. Siktberg

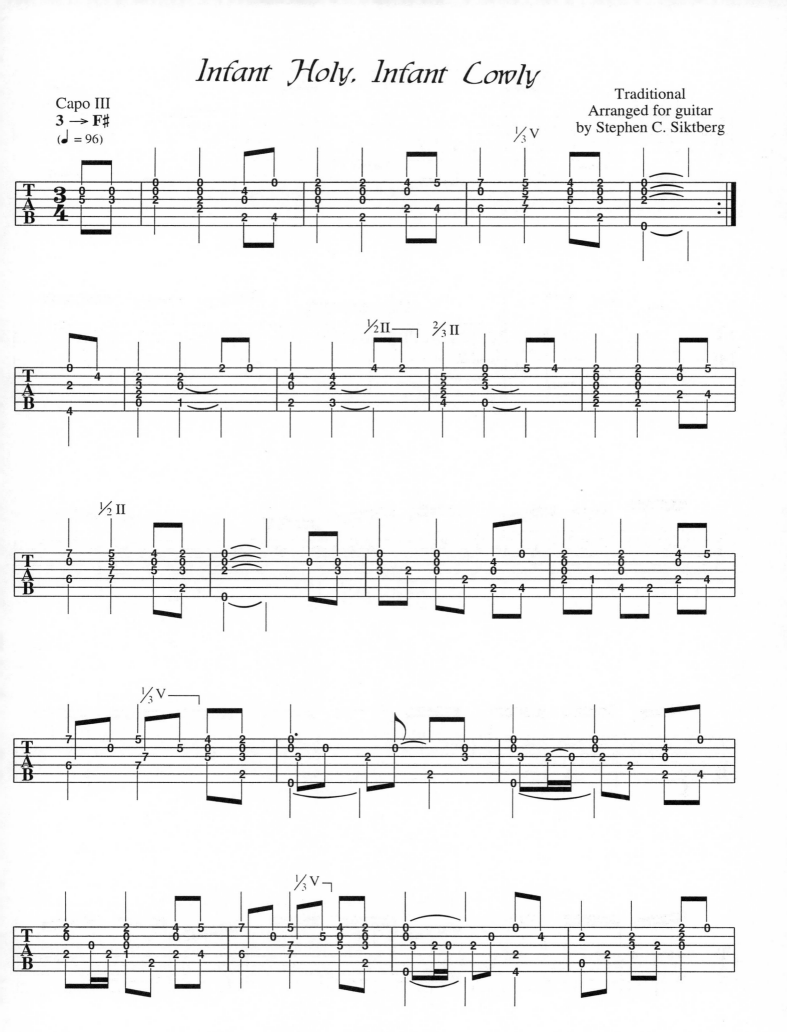

67

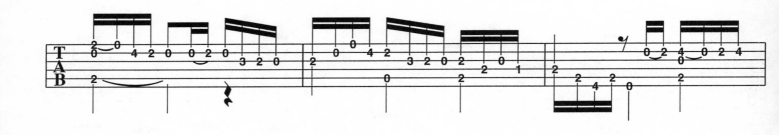

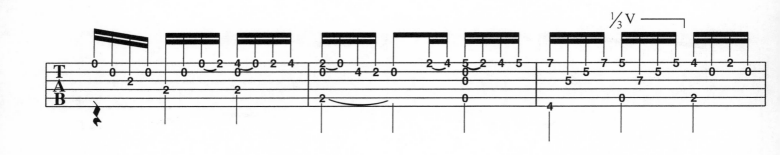

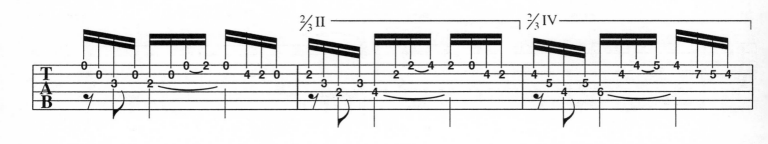

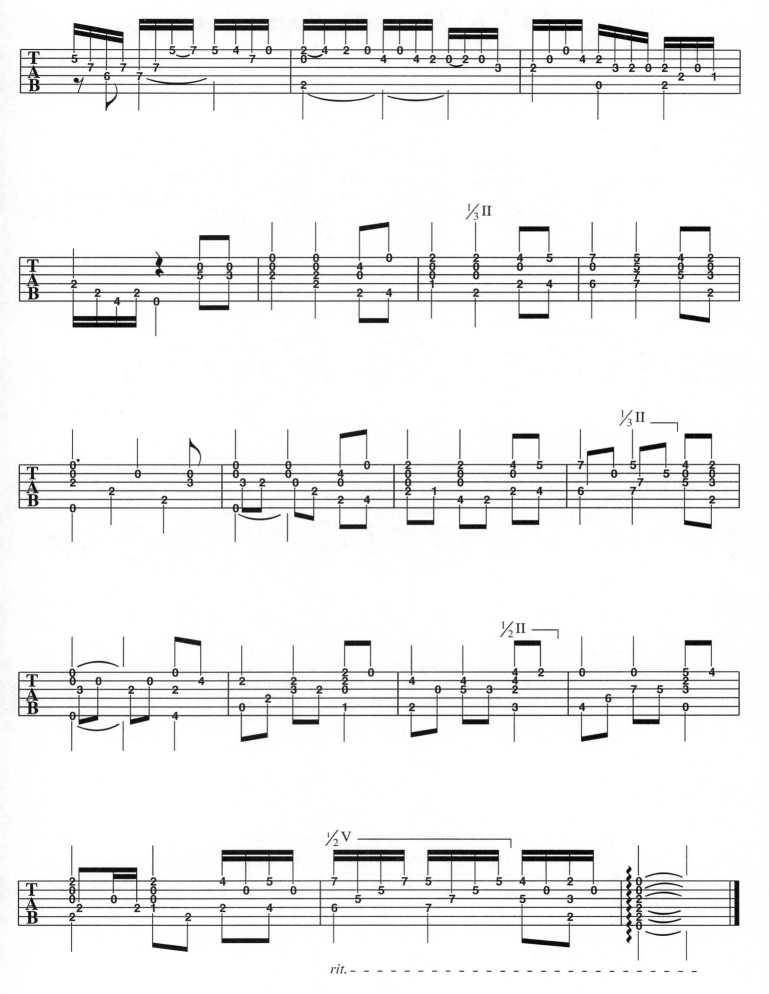

What Child Is This/We Three Kings . . .

Traditional
John H. Hopkins
Arranged for guitar
by Stephen C. Siktberg

Traditional

Dolce

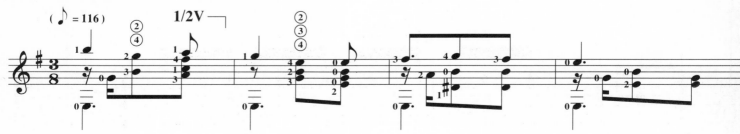

We Three Kings

What Child ...

(♪ = 108)

What Child Is This/We Three Kings . . .

Traditional
John H. Hopkins
Arranged for guitar
by Stephen C. Siktberg

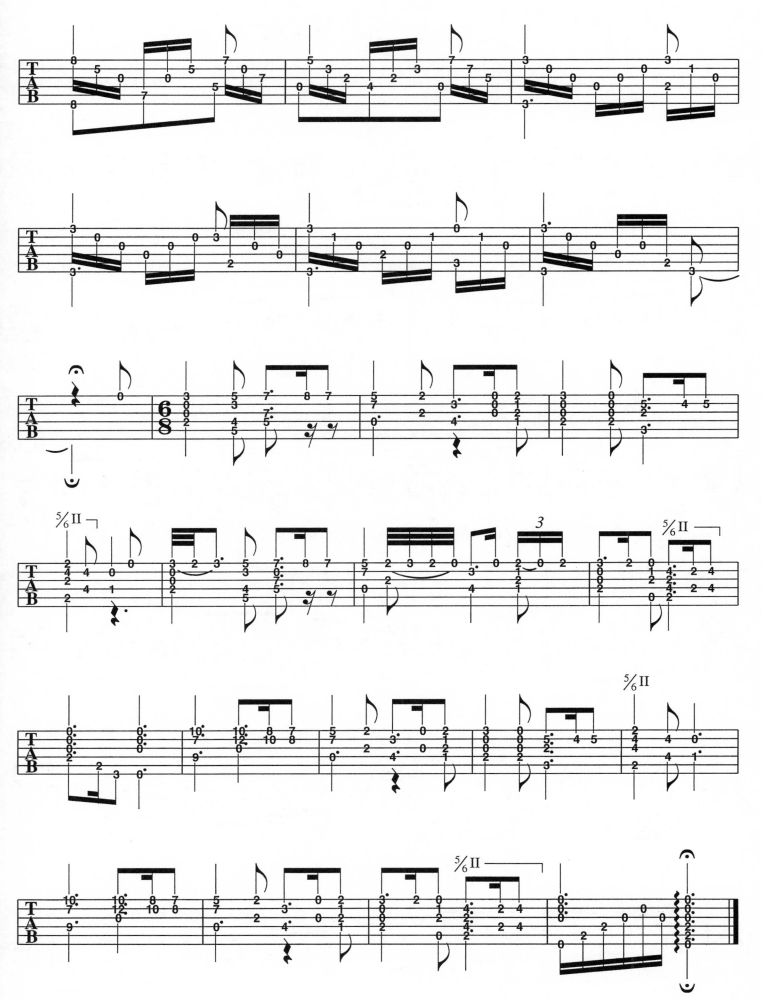

Joy to the World

G. F. Handel
Arranged for guitar
by Stephen C. Siktberg

Joy to the World

G. F. Handel
Arranged for guitar
by Stephen C. Siktberg

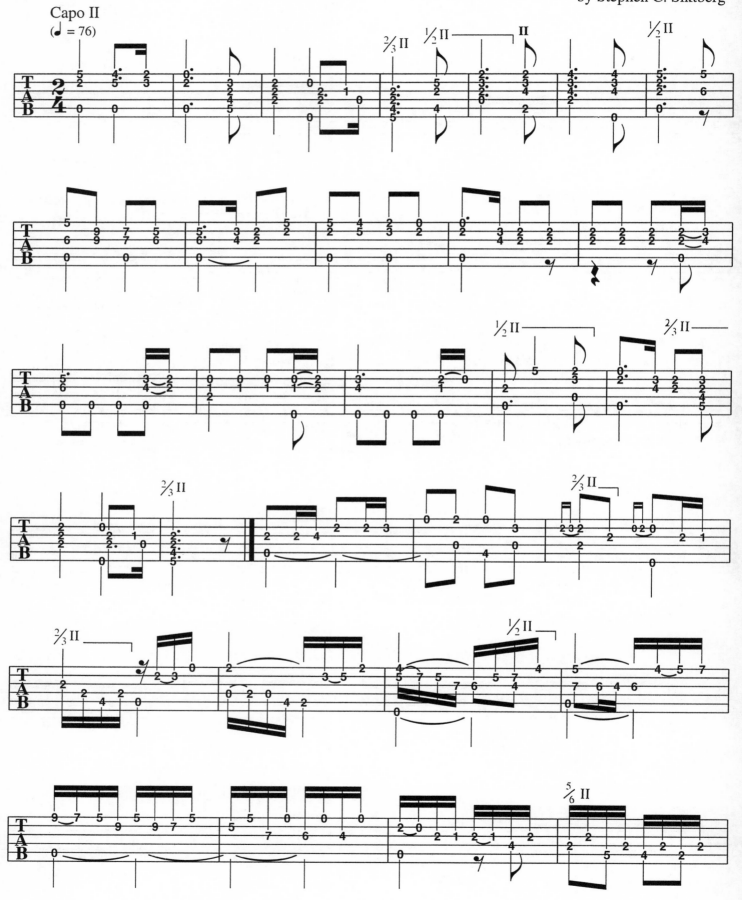

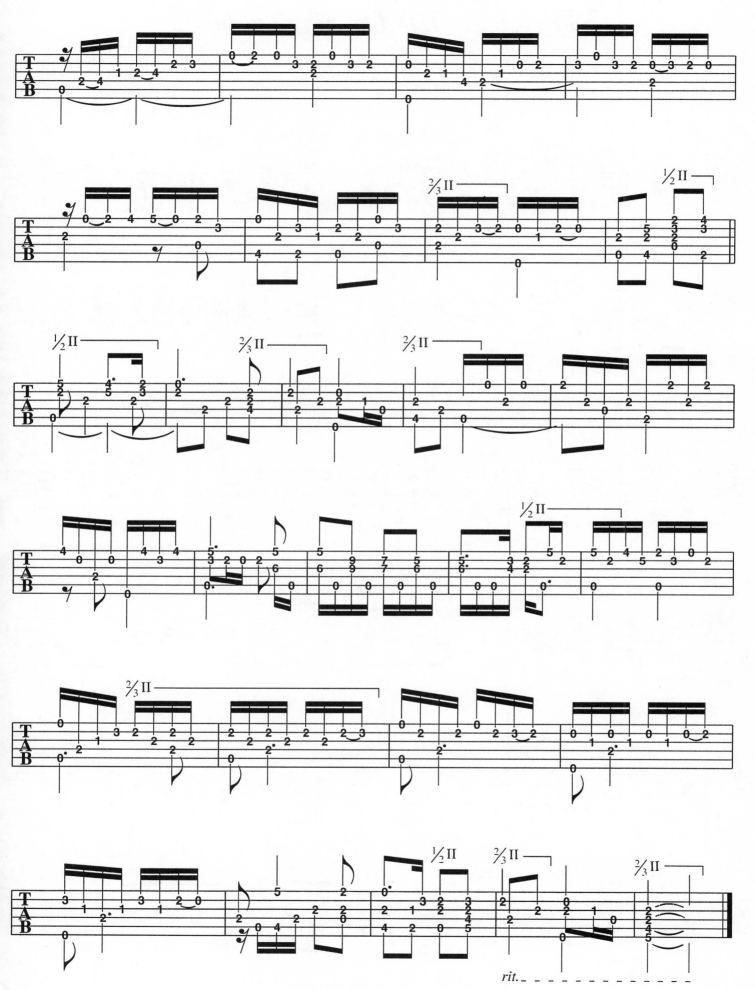

Watchman, Tell Us of the Night

Joseph Parry
Arranged for guitar
by Stephen C. Siktberg

Watchman, Tell Us of the Night

Joseph Parry
Arranged for guitar
by Stephen C. Siktberg

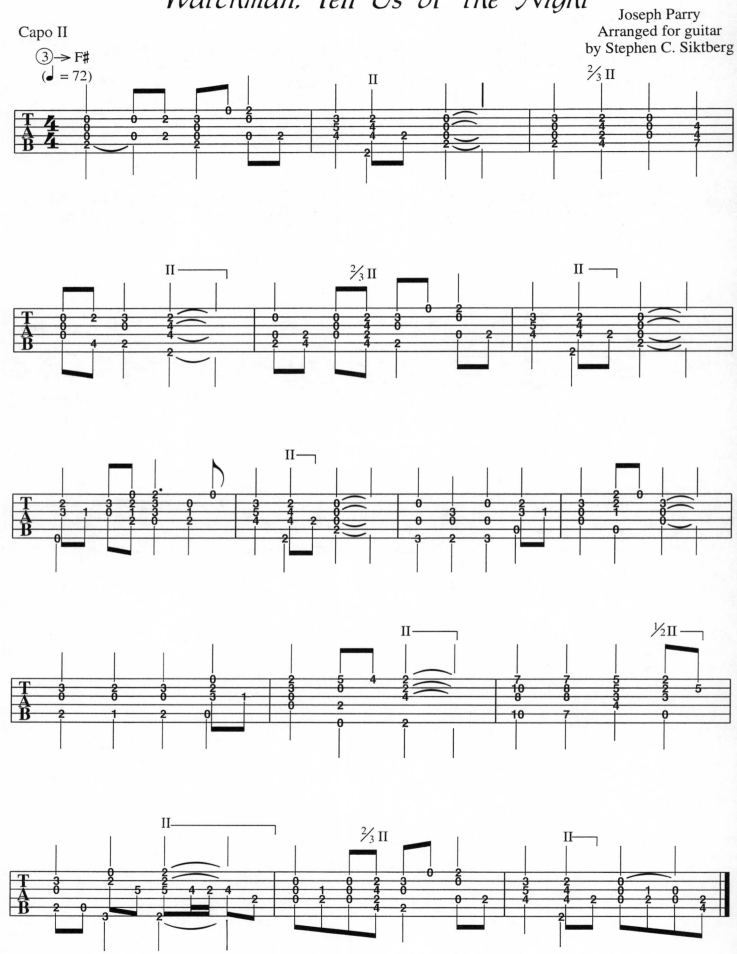

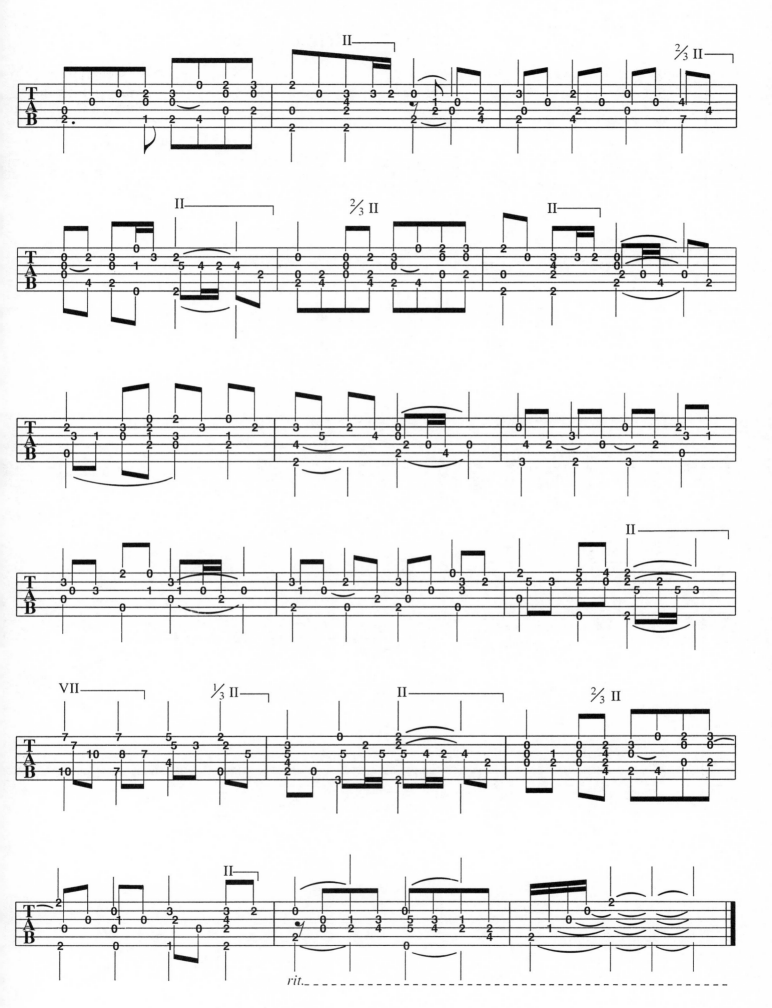

Gentle Mary

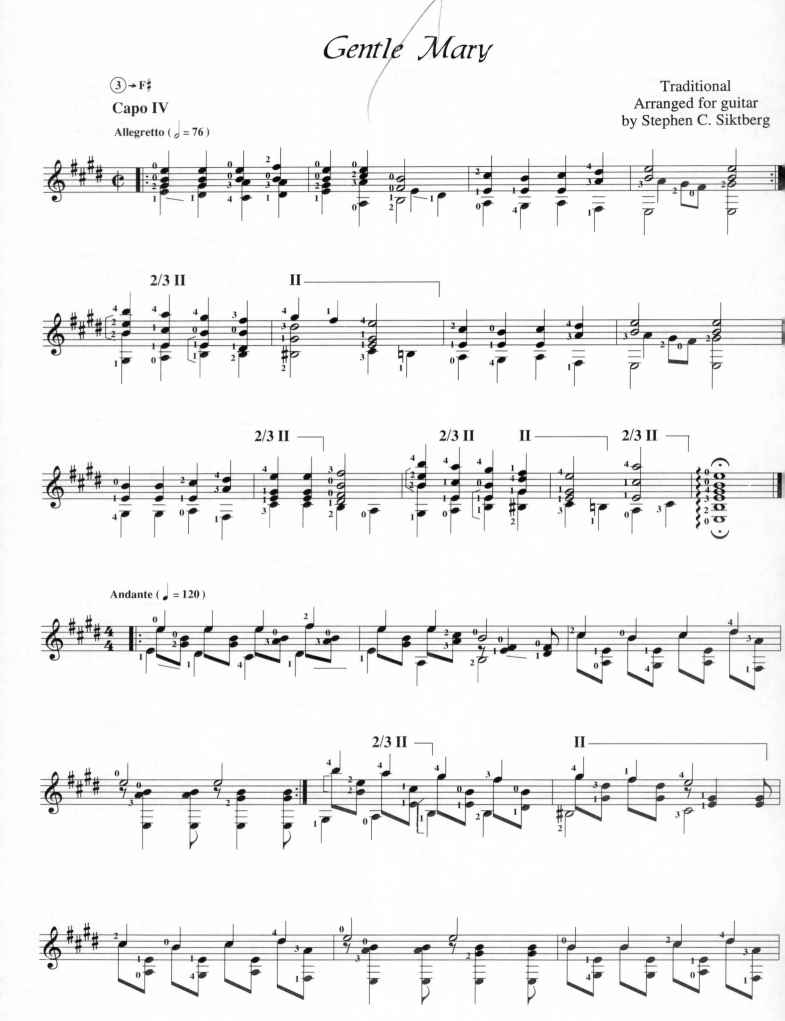

Traditional
Arranged for guitar
by Stephen C. Siktberg

Gentle Mary

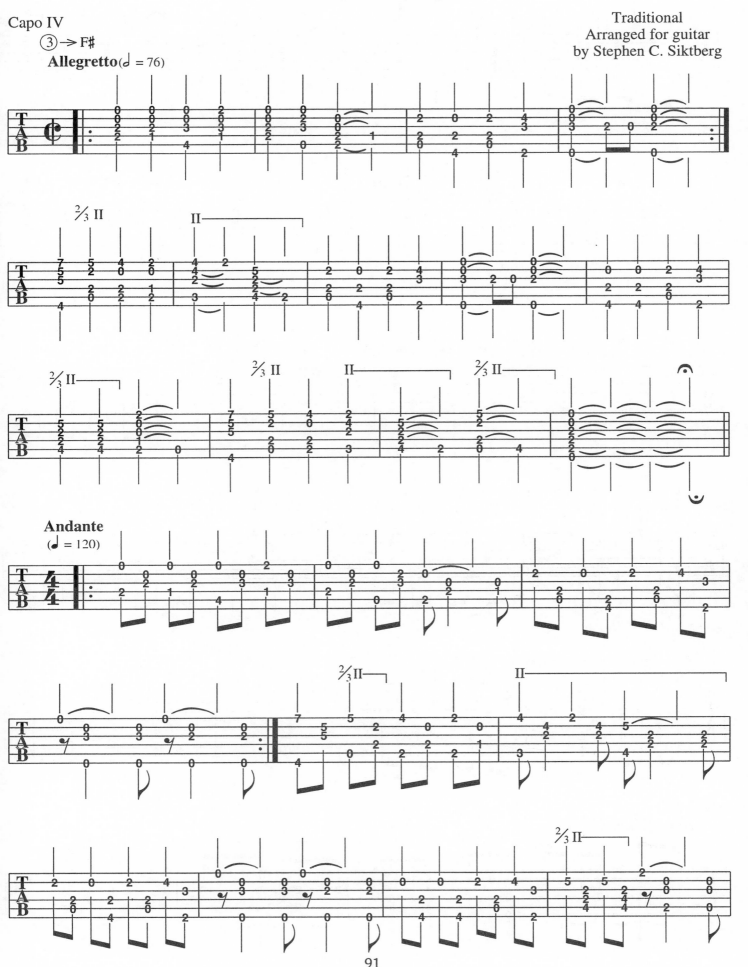

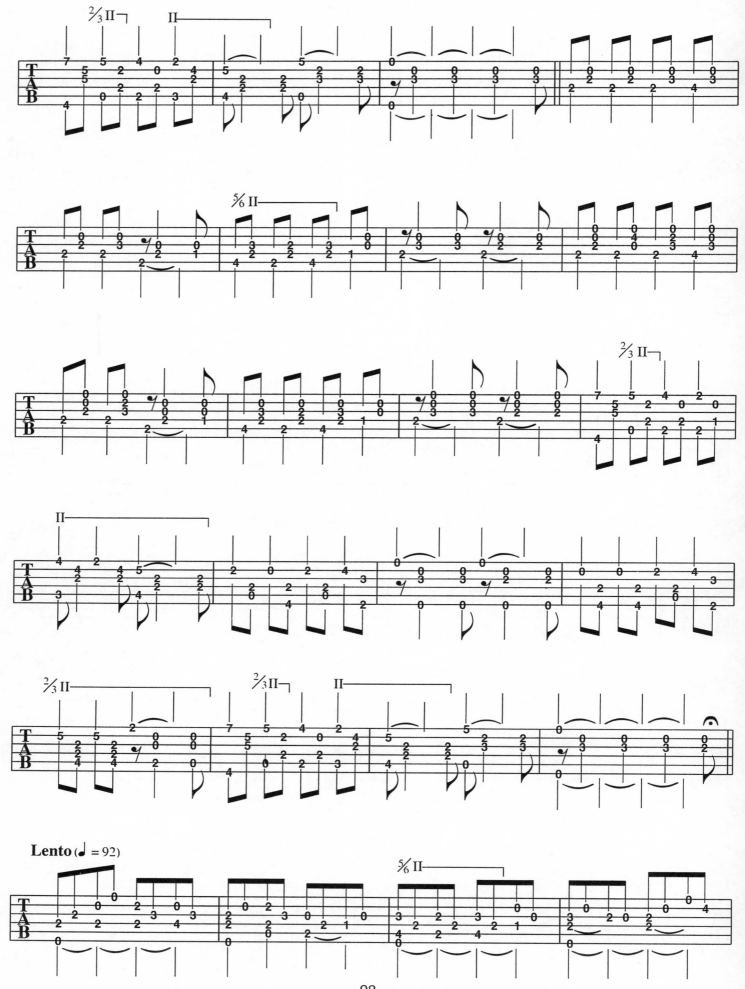

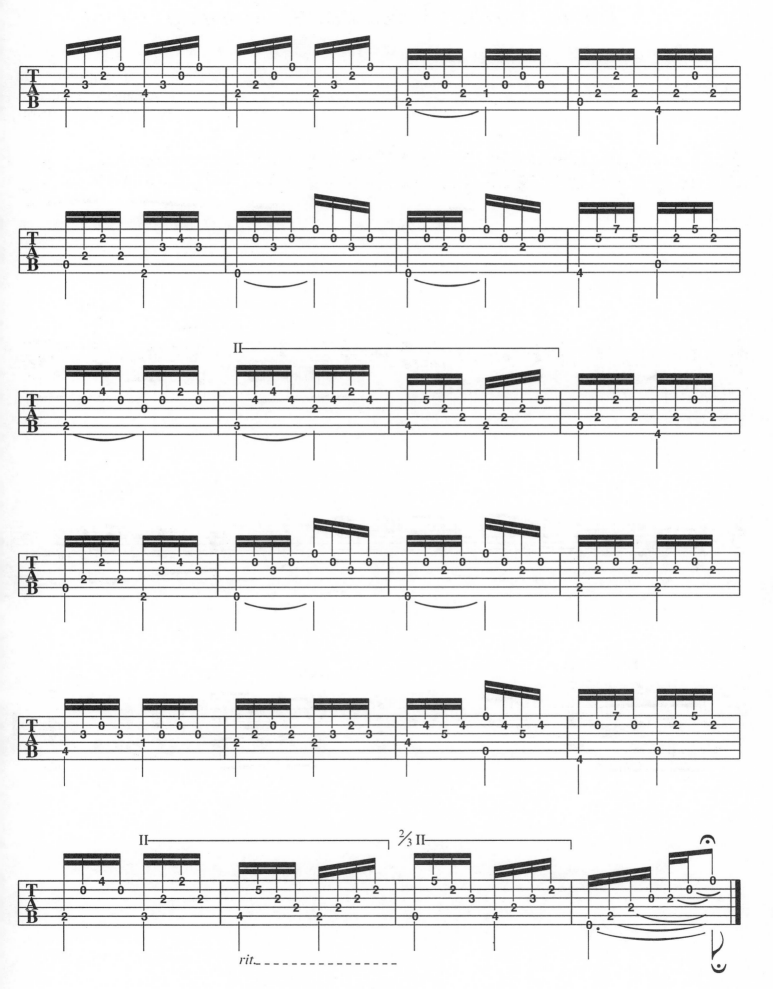

Break Forth, O Beauteous Morning Light

J. S. Bach
Arranged for guitar
by Stephen C. Siktberg

Capo I

(♩ = 80)

Break Forth, O Beauteous Morning Light

J. S. Bach
Arranged for guitar
by Stephen C. Siktberg

Capo I

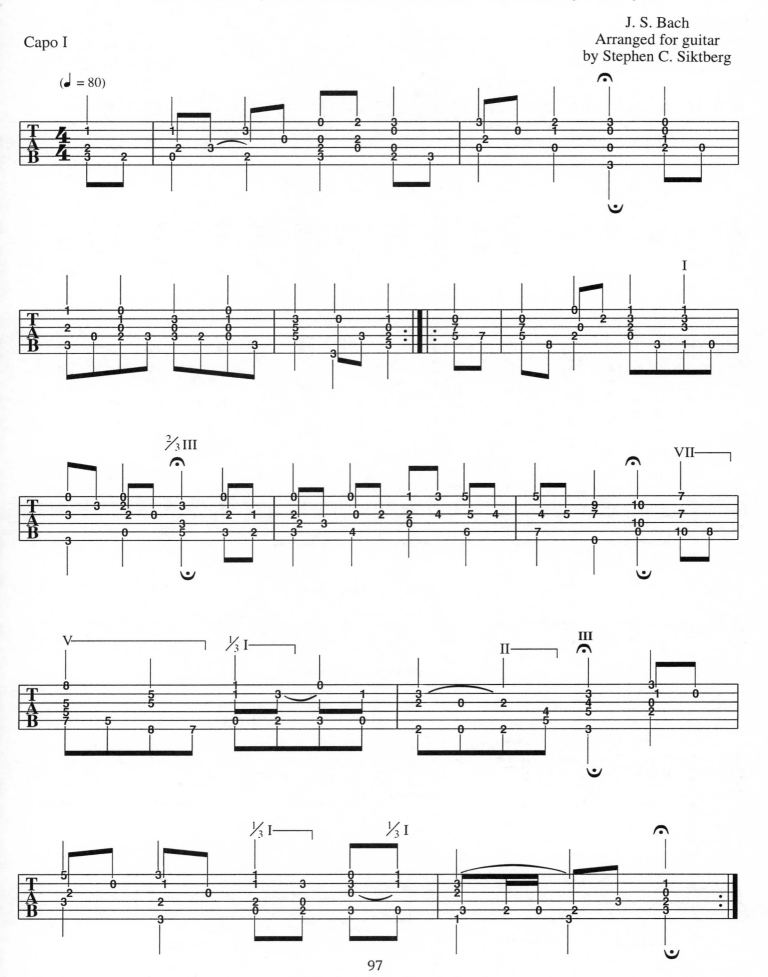

Angels From the Realms of Glory

H. T. Smart
Arranged for guitar
by Stephen C. Siktberg

While Shepherds Watched Their Flocks

G. F. Handel
Arranged for guitar
by Stephen C. Siktberg

Capo II

poco rit -

While Shepherds Watched Their Flocks

G. F. Handel
Arranged for guitar
by Stephen C. Siktberg

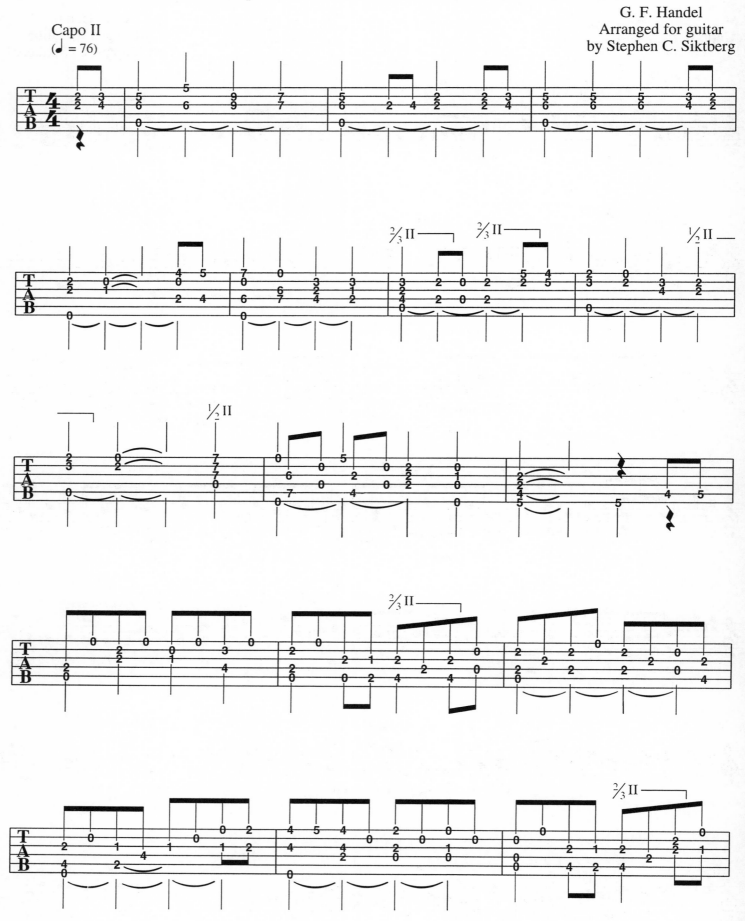

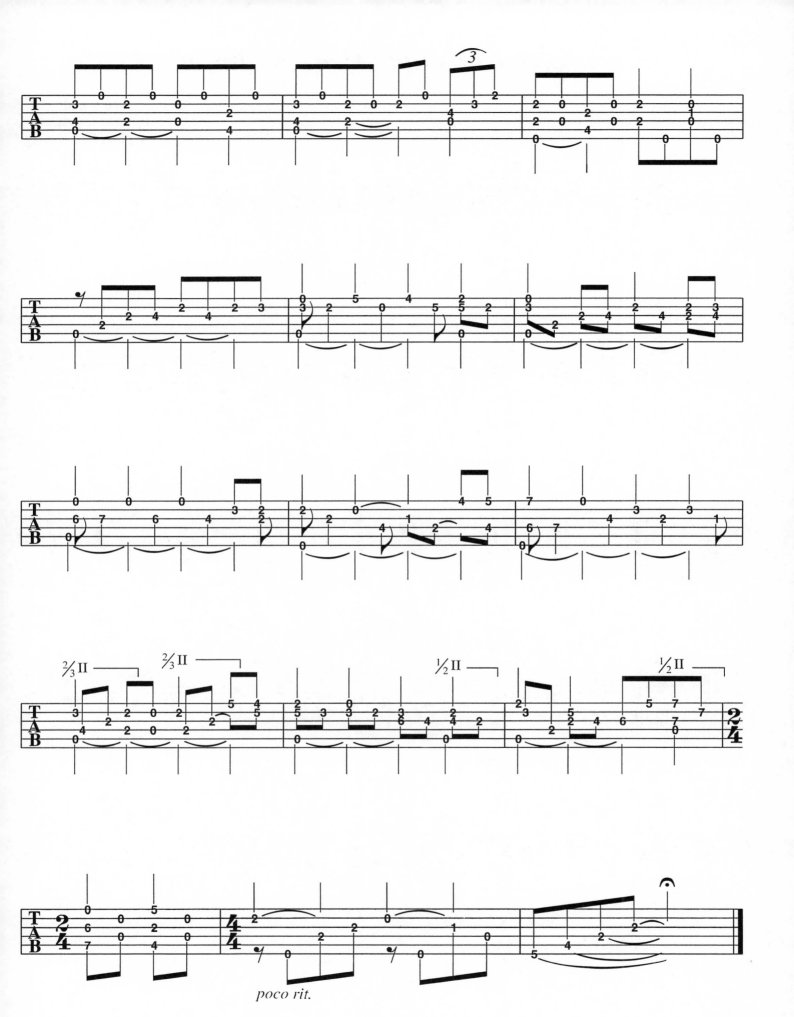

poco rit.

Good Christian Men, Rejoice!

Traditional
Arranged for guitar
by Stephen C. Siktberg

Capo III

108

Bring the Torch Jeanette, Isabella (Traditional)

109

Good Christian Men ...

Good Christian Men,...

Adagio (♩ = 100)

poco rit. _ _ _ _ _ _ 113

Silent Night

Franz Gruber
Arranged for guitar
by Stephen C. Siktberg

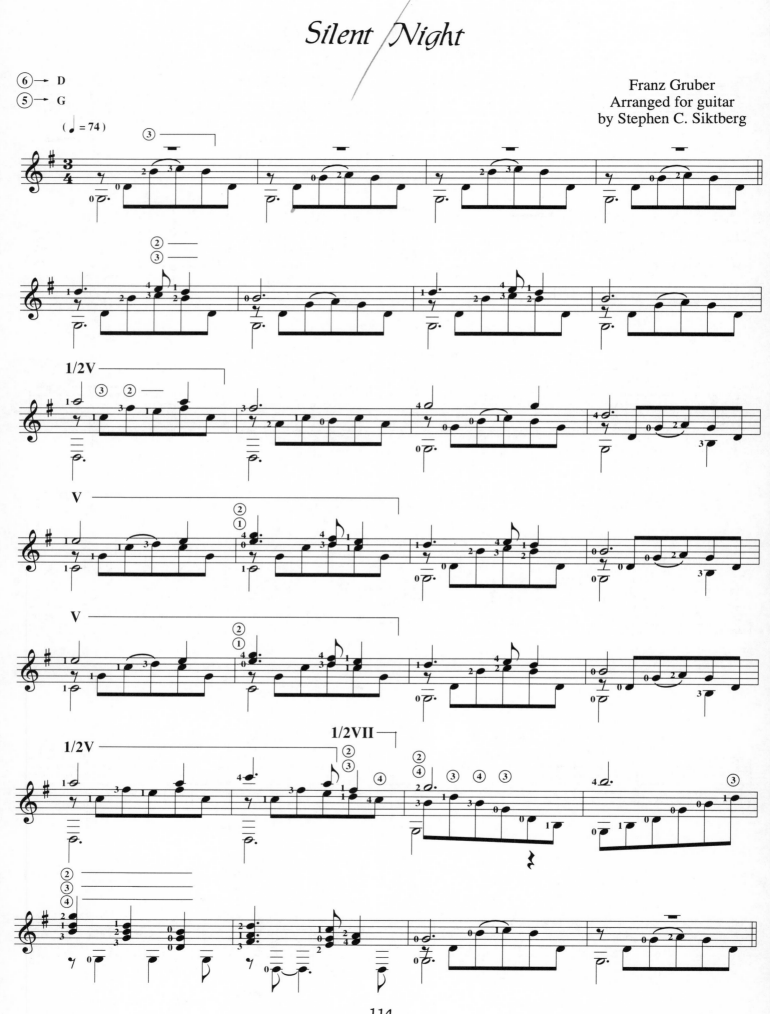

114

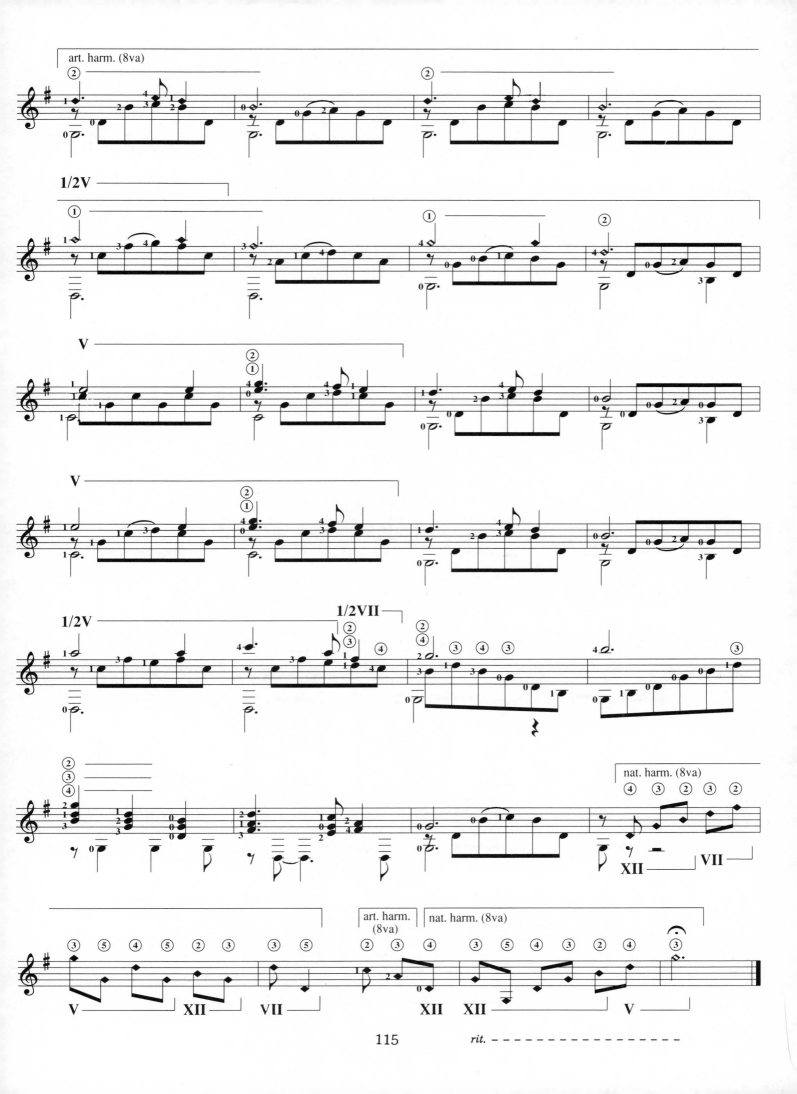

Silent Night

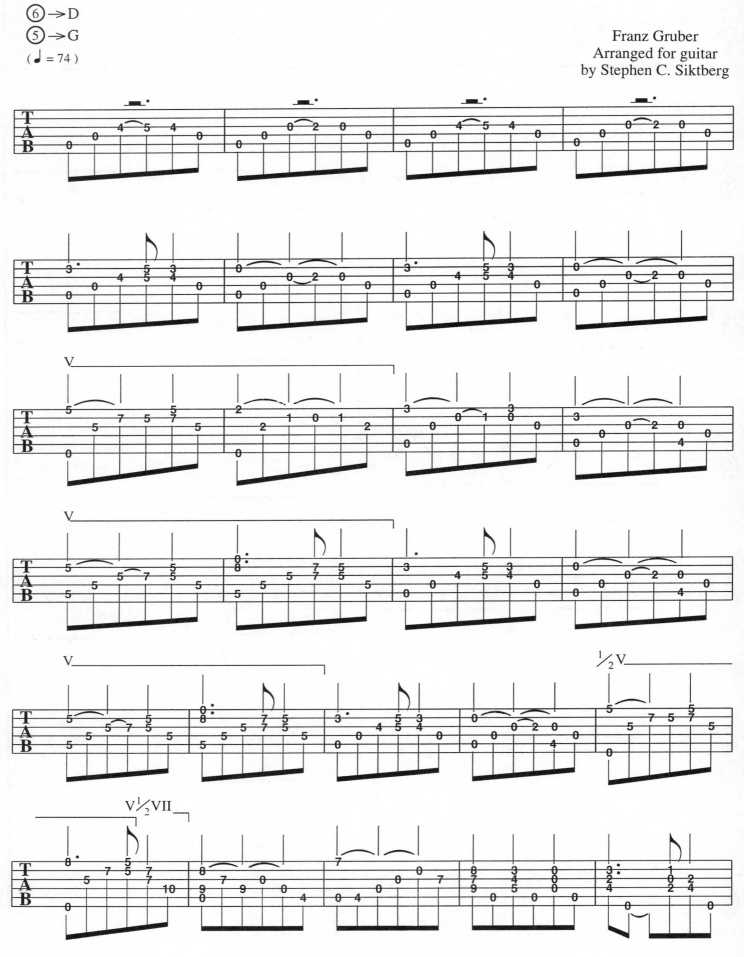

Franz Gruber
Arranged for guitar
by Stephen C. Siktberg

Great Music at Your Fingertips